CTHULHU TAKE THE WHEEL

The Collected Advice Columns of 

Vol. 7

PATRICK THOMAS

PADWOLF
PUBLISHING

PADWOLF PUBLISHING INC.
WWW.PADWOLF.COM
www.facebook.com/Padwolf

WWW.PATTHOMAS.NET
WWW.DEARCTHULHU.COM

www.facebook.com/PatrickThomasAuthor

I_PatrickThomas @ Twitter

CTHULHU TAKE THE WHEEL
The Collected Advice Columns of Dear Cthulhu Vol. 3

© 2025 Patrick Thomas

This is the first time these letters have been in print form.

Book edited by John L. French

Cover Art and Design by Patrick Thomas

Dear Cthulhu is © & TM Patrick Thomas

ISBN13 digit 978-1-958310-09-0
First printing. Printed in the USA

If you have any additional questions that Cthulhu can answer, and Cthulhu can answer all questions, Dear Cthulhu welcomes letters and questions at DearCthulhu@ dearcthulhu.com. All letters become the property of Dear Cthulhu and may be used in future columns. Sending financial offerings along with your questions is not necessary but is always appreciated.

Anyone foolish enough to follow Dear Cthulhu's advice does so at their own peril.

Cthulhu dedicates this book to himself for no others
are as worthy or deserving.

*(And after advising humanity for 20 years, Cthulhu
has more than earned it.)*

Cthulhu will one day rise up
to claim the Earth and its inhabitants as his own.
The Great Old One has looked
upon Humankind and found it lacking.
Cthulhu has deemed it necessary
to prepare Humankind for his coming
Thus, Cthulhu now answers humanity's questions
to help them better themselves
to one day better serve him.

Dear Cthulhu,

I'm fresh out of mortician school. I went into the profession because my uncle owns a funeral home. He doesn't have any kids and wants the business to stay in the family because when it's his time, he doesn't want to be worked on by a stranger.

It was a big honor and kind of a relief because I never really knew what I wanted to do for a living. I'm a bit on the lazy side. I can handle almost any work that's put in front of me, but I don't go looking for it.

I'd been working for my uncle for six months when he finally trusted me enough to take a day off, his first in two years. There was nothing major going on, just the last day of two services where both clients had been cremated.

A woman whose husband had died came in to pick up his ashes. It was one of those May–December relationships. He was in his 70s and she was in her 30s and as hot as a cremation furnace. She was dressed in a very short, low–cut, skintight black dress. I knew something was strange when she came into the office and locked the door behind her. At first, she cried on my shoulder but before I knew it, she had my pants off and was riding me on top of my uncle's desk.

I was happy and bewildered at the same time. When she got off (of me), I yanked my pants back up and handed her the ashes. The widow went home. It was only then that I realized I'd given her the ashes of the other client, an 85–year–old woman.

Before I could figure out what to do, the woman's children came for her ashes, so I just handed them the hot widow's husband's remains. In all fairness, it was a bit confusing since both urns looked identical–we were running a special since they were last year's model.

I felt terrible and the last thing I wanted was for my uncle to find out how badly I'd screwed up. That night, I figured I'd go see the widow and explain that after our mutual grieving, I'd mixed things up. I'd ask for the ashes back, then visit the dead woman's family, apologize, and make the exchange.

When I knocked on the widow's door, she greeted me in skimpy lingerie while fanning herself with a handful of money. Before I could say anything, she grabbed me by the tie and I had the most amazing night of my life. I didn't leave till morning. The subject of the mistake with the ashes never came up, although other things did.

I still felt guilty, so I went back every night for a week hoping to tell her what happened and finally make the exchange, but every night we never got to the point where we'd actually talk. After that week, she left for a singles' cruise, followed by a world cruise. She's not going to be back for four months. It makes no sense for me to go to the other family and tell them about the error if I can't give them the correct ashes.

My uncle has no idea and thinks I did a great job. My worry is, should I come clean to my uncle, then when the widow gets back make the exchange? Or should I just let it go? The odds are very low either family will ever have the ashes tested and even if they do, it is difficult to test cremains, so there is maybe a one in a million chance of my error being found out by anyone. And honestly, I'm pretty sure the widow would understand why I was distracted. From the impression I got, I don't think it would bother her much.

Should I fess up to my uncle or keep my mouth shut?
–Undertaker In An Unusual Undertaking In Utah

Dear Undertaker,

At this point, it does not seem like you would do anything but upset the family members and possibly ruin your position at your uncle's mortuary. Keep your mouth shut and if anything does ever come up, you can say it was your first day by yourself and you got a bit flustered. Most people will understand. People are foolish that way.

Dear Cthulhu,

I'm in love with the most wonderful woman in the world. We just got married, so I'm in heaven. I've been in love with my wife for over 11 years, which is a good 10 years before we officially met. I'd been admiring her from afar for a decade. Well, not always so far. I knew what hours she worked and would break into her apartment to feel closer to her, sneaking quick naps while using her dirty socks and underwear as a pillow.

"Millie" is an old–fashioned girl who even keeps a diary, which I was fortunate enough to read during the times I broke into her apartment. The secrets held within that sacred tome are what led to us getting together. That and Fate of course. Millie had broken up with her latest loser boyfriend and wrote that she was glad to be rid of him and how she hoped she could just find a nice guy who could make her laugh.

Well, I'm a nice guy and if I'd have managed to get a hold of a tank of nitrous oxide like I planned, I could've made her laugh like nobody's business.

I "accidentally" bumped into her at her favorite coffee shop. Not that it was the first time I'd seen her there. In fact, I'd been directly in front of or behind her in line nearly a hundred times and my poor clueless love never noticed me, but I made sure that day was going to be different. I started off making small talk about the weather, then asked her out for coffee. She pointed out that she was already having coffee and that, no, she didn't want to get coffee another time with me. I was so devastated by her rejection and denial of our obvious and true love that I didn't break into her apartment for two days. When I did, I found I'd finally made it into those blessed pages, although it wasn't very flattering. She wrote how a not terribly attractive guy had had the nerve to ask her out. There's no mention of how nice I was or the fact that I had actually paid for her coffee and even had them throw in the type of scone that she likes. It was the Spacebucks where the manager got his job by winning a contest with his own blend of coffee, and we both got that special.

Then I realized what her problem was. Millie was so concerned with physical appearance that she couldn't see the value of a person whom she didn't find attractive. I was in love with Millie and wasn't about to give up on her and our great romance just because of a simple rejection and her dimwitted inability to realize what was best for her.

Once I figured her out, the solution to ending our painful separation was quite obvious. I knew what I had to do to get Millie to love me. I had to break down the beauty barrier between us.

I had options. Get a makeover, work out for a few months, or get cosmetic surgery. When I thought about the time, effort and expense all these would involve, I realized my looks weren't the problem. *I* was fine. Millie was the problem.

The main reason my lady love thought I wasn't attractive was because she could *see* me. If that little detail was no longer in the way, Millie would finally see what a wonderful person I was. Well, I guess I should say realize.

I did what any reasonable man in love would do. I laced her contacts with a slow-acting acid, so the next time she wore them Millie lost her eyesight.

Millie was devastated. I visited her in the hospital, but she didn't recognize me. Obviously. I told her I was a volunteer at the hospital. I visited to talk and read her passages from her favorite books, which coincidentally happened to be my favorites too. When she got out, I was there to take her home. I helped teach her how to get around and assisted her when she needed it. I hired actors to speak loudly in her vicinity about how sad and hideous she looked without any eyes and how handsome I was. The constant cries of disgust wherever she went gradually eroded her confidence in herself. To make a long and very romantic story short, I wore her down and she agreed to marry me. It's been simply wonderful.

There's one catch. On our honeymoon, which I told her was at an exclusive resort but only down the shore, she whispered how grateful she was for me, that we should always tell each other the truth, and that we should have no lies between us. Like ever. Her words made me feel very icky inside. I did not care for it one bit. If I had to guess, this inner turmoil is what others call guilt.

I didn't ever plan to tell her how I had arranged for our love to blossom, but now that we're husband and wife, I want to abide by her wishes.

But I'm not quite sure if I had really lied to Millie as I'd never told her it hadn't been me who arranged for her to go blind. Am I merely guilty of omission, or did I lie by not telling her? Should I come clean and tell her the truth? I don't know if our love is strong enough to survive that much honesty.

–Man Who Proved Love Is Blind In Bethesda

Dear Bethesda,

The answer to your dilemma depends on the interpretation of lied. While you did not tell an untruth, you have not shared the whole truth either. The omission is rather significant. Were you to tell her what you did, your marriage would likely be over and you would be looking at significant jail time.

There are other factors to consider. As regular readers well know, Cthulhu takes vows quite seriously. Cthulhu has worshipers who make vows to him. When other humans break their vows, it can give my worshippers the idea that they can follow suit. Dissuading my flock from doing this would take up a great deal of time on my part and involve much discomfort and maiming for them.

You vowed to love, honor, cherish, and protect your wife. But remember, you made these vows *after* you maimed her. In order to keep these vows, you must never harm her again. Sadly, because of your actions, Millie needs help to take care of herself and you appear to be the only person who stepped up. Although this is a twisted and sad truth, you make her existence easier by helping her which is the only reason I haven't sent my worshippers to forcibly invite you to be the guest of honor at our next human sacrifice.

As long as you maintain your vows, it appears that she will have a less difficult time navigating her life with you than without you. Because of this, Cthulhu recommends keeping the omission to yourself. And should you ever leave her, rest assured you will end up as a ritual sacrifice to the greater glory of Cthulhu.

Dear Cthulhu,

I'm a big fan of windmills. In fact, you could say I love them. Sometimes a bit too literally. I live in a town that has a bunch of wind farms. You can see the row of windmills from miles away. They're majestic, a mix of futuristic science fiction and retro Middle Ages. When I'm driving through town along the highway and see them, I get aroused. It's gotten to where I find the windmills more attractive than my girlfriend. Don't get me wrong. She's a pretty woman and my best friend, but in a choice between her in a skimpy negligée and an elegant windmill with its blades spinning in the breeze, my girlfriend's going to lose every time. We moved six months ago and before that, our love life was fine. Then we moved, I saw the windmills, and suddenly "Wendy" wasn't enough for me anymore. When we moved in, we were having sex two or three times a day, but it was winter. The leaves had fallen off the trees and I could see the windmills from the window in our bedroom. Now, it's spring and leaves are in my line of sight, so there's been no nooky for the last couple of months.

My urges didn't go away, but it's not like I can ask Wendy to dress up in a windmill outfit in the bedroom. It got so bad I couldn't sleep. Every time I rolled over, I was like a bike with a kickstand down, if you get my drift.

I got out of bed in the middle of the night and went for a bicycle ride. I ended up in the hills where a wind farm is. I'd never actually been there before. It's pretty deserted and there are trees all around, so you can't see the bottom of the main shaft. Plus, it was dark and two in the morning, so I hugged a windmill. And as is apt to happen with these sorts of things, the hugging led to heavy petting, which led to… Well, let's just say that before you know it, I'd consummated my love of windmills.

When I got home, I felt like a freak, but slept like a baby.

I've been sneaking out almost every night since. Last night Wendy noticed and confronted me when I got back. She thinks I'm cheating on her and she's not exactly wrong. I told her the truth, that there was no other woman in my life but her. Honestly, Wendy is perfect for me in every way except I have this bizarre fetish.

What can I do to make both Wendy and me happy in the bedroom department?

–Don Juan Quixote in Davenport

Dear Don,

Do not feel like a freak. Trust Cthulhu on this. One would not believe some of the bizarre and depraved letters I get from people whose fetishes are far worse than yours:

–a woman who has to glue fizzing antacids to her skin and go out in the rain with a man who rolled first in butter then coffee grounds while wearing a clown mask

– a man who needed a chainsaw, chickens, and a pool of lime gelatin to consummate his marriage

– a club for men who violate the tailpipes of cars while dressed as train engineers

– and one poor fellow who couldn't get aroused unless his lover dressed on his left side like Eleanor Roosevelt and Abraham Lincoln on the other.

Anyone who cared enough to try would no doubt trace your obsession back to something that happened in your childhood, which through the pathetic workings of the human mind transferred itself into your adult psyche. Cthulhu will not waste your time with that sort of thing because it would take years and tens of thousands of dollars to even hope to come to terms with any of it.

In the end, the fact that you have urges that cause you to be aroused by windmills will likely never be extinguished entirely. Instead of wasting years of your life and a small fortune to ultimately fail, Cthulhu is going to help you to cope and flourish within the boundaries of your particular depravity.

You write in your letter that it is not like you can ask your girlfriend to dress up like a windmill. Why not? If you have an open and loving relationship, you should be able to talk about anything with her. You say she is your best friend and your perfect match in every other way. Approach her with the idea. Perhaps she would consider getting a tattoo of a windmill to help or a hat with a tiny working version atop it.

Another way to spice up your procreation time is to tell her you have a fantasy about the two of you procreating by the windmills. The pair of you could take your bikes up to the wind farm. You could put her up against the windmill so that when you procreate, you can touch her and the windmill. Be creative and you will likely be able to satisfy both of your procreational needs.

You don't mention your financial status, but perhaps you can purchase some land and build a windmill of your own in an isolated area where the two of you can procreate to your loins' content. Make sure to place it in an area where you can see it from multiple windows in the house. Place models, pictures, even holographic art of modern windmills through the house so you can use one for inspiration and stimulation when you and your wife mate. Just try not to make it obvious when you are procreating that you are staring out the windows instead of at her, because much of my correspondence from women complains about their men not paying enough attention to them.

Dear Cthulhu,

I've always felt that I was born into the wrong body. I'm a 24-year-old man who clocks in at four foot ten, one hundred and eight-pound, but in my heart, I know I'm a six foot ten three-hundred-pound Viking berserker.

The problem is no one will take me seriously. My brother used to be my sister and everyone's okay with that. Which I might add is how it should be, but when I came out to my family to tell them I was really a Viking, they just looked at me funny. When my then-sister said she wanted to become a man, after the initial shock, there were hugs and crying and promises of unconditional love and support. Me? They said to grow up and get over it.

Not only did my parents help with the cost of everything my former sister needed to do to become my brother, but they even got him a lawyer when his employer gave him grief. They wouldn't give me a dime towards getting hair plugs on my face and chest so I'd have a thicker beard and finally have body hair. Forget about getting me any battle armor, even though I said it was the only thing I wanted for Christmas and my birthday. When I suggested I was going to start taking anabolic steroids to bulk up, I got a lecture on the dangers involved. I mean my brother can do everything that he needed to do to become his true self, so shouldn't I be entitled to be a hairy warrior raping and pillaging my way through life?

I don't think it's fair. What can I do to make my parents treat me as well as they treat my brother? Or do you think it's because they like him better?

–Viking in Vancouver

Dear Vancouver,

First off, Cthulhu is not human and even Cthulhu can tell that the two things you are comparing are not the same. Not being able to live out the make-believe idea of being something that you probably don't know much about and only have a fantasized view of is not the same as feeling you have been born the wrong gender. Cthulhu wonders if you had this desire prior to your sibling sharing the information or if perhaps your reaction is just a way of trying to compensate for feeling that you were getting less love and being ignored by those who gave you birth.

And no, you do not have an inherent right to actually rape or pillage. If you want to bulk up your musculoskeletal system and grow a beard because you feel that would make you look more attractive to a possible mate, go ahead. That makes sense. But to think you are going to do in the modern age what you fantasize Vikings did centuries ago is beyond foolhardy. The authorities would simply take you into custody. Or if your violent acting out became bad enough, they would simply take you down during your crimes. The Scots and Irish did not have automatic weapons or the Vikings would have been wiped out fairly quickly.

However, there are many ways the modern human can pillage, many of them in the corporate world. Corporate raiders buy up floundering companies and sell them off piecemeal in much the same way Vikings did to villages. They make cuts to and fire both management and workers to increase the value of a company. You can ruin someone's life without using a weapon. It is likely the closest thing to a Viking in the modern world.

On the off chance that this is truly a deep-seated desire rather than delusional fantasy fulfillment, there are more socially acceptable ways to indulge yourself. There is an activity known as cosplaying, where people dress up as their favorite characters from movies, books, and even historical periods. It might take some searching, but there are groups out there dedicated to Viking activities. Join them and you can have fun dressing up and attending their events, renaissance fairs, and even fantasy conventions. There are realistic feasts and contests that could allow you to indulge your desires. Often when in costume, people in these groups can even take different names so you could get yourself a Viking name, act like a Viking (without hurting another human as all humans shall one day be Cthulhu's and I do not appreciate my property being damaged by anyone other than me), and all around pretend to be a Viking so you can live in a manner which will allow you to function in society the rest of the time.

To answer your final question, Cthulhu is unfamiliar with your family, but from what you wrote, I think it is quite possible that your parents do care for your sibling more than you. Although that perception may be due less to any transitioning or wanting–to–be–a–Viking than your perceived personality.

Dear Cthulhu,

I've never had much luck with women. I don't think I'm unattractive but I've never had a woman interested in me. At least as far as I know.

I've tried to learn how to meet and pick up women by watching TV, movies, and the Internet. I've used pickup lines, everything from *What's your sign?* to *How about you and I get out of here and go back to your place?* Because I saw it in a movie, I even asked one woman if she wanted to come back to my place to see my etchings. She asked me what etchings were and I didn't know so it didn't work out that time. In fact, none of those lines did. The responses have varied from *Get the hell away from me!* (In retrospect asking a woman at a wake if she comes here often probably wasn't the best timing or choice of line) to being slapped across the face then whipped with rosary beads until I bled. Again in retrospect, telling a nun on the bus that I had a serpent that wanted to enter her Garden of Eden was a horrible idea. I just figured maybe she'd like the bible angle and give me a shot.

I turned to porn for inspiration. I mean the guys in those movies do amazing with the ladies. I mean they barely even have to say anything before the clothes come off and the nookie starts.

I got a job as a pizza delivery guy but not once did any nubile or even unnubile woman meet me at the door in lingerie to ask if there was some way she could compensate me for the pizza because she didn't have any money to pay with. Part of that may be due to the fact that most people order online and pay with a credit card but still.

I started looking at houses to buy but no real estate agent ever offered to sweeten the deal by breaking in the house's bed with me. I begged my parents to get divorced and remarried so I'd have a stepmother and some stepsisters but they selfishly refused because they were "happily" married.

I had just about given up when I saw the internet debate about whether a woman would prefer to meet a man or a bear in the woods. It turns out most of them prefer the bear.

To be honest, I didn't even know the woods were a place that woman went to meet men or bears. I had to get in on this in hopes of meeting a woman. Despite being desperate, I really had no interest in dating a bear.

I went with the romantic approach and set up a picnic lunch with wine, bread, and assorted meats and cheeses. They were laid out artistically on top of a blanket and set up in a cleared area beside a well–used trail. I sat and waited, occasionally nibbled on cheese and crackers.

The route was very popular and a good many people hiked or jogged along it. A few even use mountain bikes. I sat, ignoring the men or women who were in the company of others, figuring that women with men were probably together. Plus the man might take offense if I hit on his partner. If women were with other women–assuming they were not together romantically–it would be awkward for me to choose between them, especially when trying to figure out which one might actually be interested in having a picnic date with me.

It took a little while but I finally found a woman walking through the woods by herself. She was quite a bit older than I was and definitely not the most attractive woman that had passed by, but she was the first one who was alone.

I stepped out and said hello. She awkwardly slowed down and took an ear bud out of one year.

"Do you need something?" she said.

"Just someone to share this lovely picnic with," I replied.

Misunderstanding me, she said, "I'm sure your date will appreciate it when she gets here."

I decided to go for broke and said, "Actually, I think you're the one I've been waiting for."

This did not go over well. She pulled pepper spray out of her pocket and pointed it at me as she ran away. I could hear her talking through her earbuds to what I can only assume was 911 and telling them to send the police because a strange man was lurking in the woods waiting for women who were alone.

My first reaction was that I better get out of the woods as I wouldn't want to bump into somebody like that before I realized she was talking about me.

The sheer ingratitude. Here I had sprung for mid–level wine and the best meat and cheese selection that my gas station had to offer and not only was she too good to join me in a little picnicking, she was insulting me and sending the cops after me.

Not wanting to have to explain myself to the cops, I threw all the food into the picnic basket followed by picnic blanket and took off down the opposite way down the trail and headed to my car.

That idea had been a bust but then I remembered that for some reason most women had said they would prefer to meet a bear in the woods which truthfully seemed a little odd to me as I always thought bears were dangerous and should be avoided. Still, that information gave me an idea. When my grandfather died, I ended up with a lot of furniture from his old cabin plus an old bearskin rug which didn't exactly fit with my décor. I put it in storage in my attic. I'd always made my own costumes for Halloween and do a little cosplaying so I transformed the rug into a pretty impressive–looking bear costume.

Picking a new set of woods in another town, I brought the picnic basket with me and set up the blanket with all the food and wine again, this time further back so I was hidden behind a thick tree but could still see the path. Since I was sticking with the solo woman plan, I figured it would be best not to show myself, especially if a woman decided to ditch the man they were because they got all excited about seeing a bear. The man might be upset and come after the bear which of course was really me in my bear rug costume. I didn't need that kind of drama in my life.

I waited behind the tree and watched people go by until a woman by herself came jogging down the trail.

I'd hit the jackpot. She was young, blond, gorgeous, and built like a swimsuit model. I eased alongside the path and sat down on my costume's hunches and did my best to look like a cute bear. It took a moment until the woman saw me. She stopped jogging and froze in her tracks.

The problem was, she didn't look like she wanted to meet a bear. She seemed terrified. To put her at ease, I waved a paw at her.

Instead of calming her, it made her scream. Things weren't working out like I planned so I tried to open up the costume so I could show her that she was safe but the paws were too bulky and didn't have opposable thumbs. I fumbled trying to take it off when suddenly a male jogger came up behind her. She turned and ran to him, grabbing hold of him with one arm and using the other to point at me.

"That bear is trying to eat me!"

Which was a total lie. I was about to tell the guy that when he reached under his T–shirt and pulled out a gun. It was small but even a small gun shoots bullets. I turned to leave quickly when I heard a gunshot. Sprinting into the woods, I didn't stop until I was out of sight.

This idea was a disaster and not going anything like I'd planned. Finally managing to get out of the bear costume, I folded in inside out and tip toed back towards my picnic area.

As I got closer I could hear shouting and moaning. I watched from a distance as the woman and the man were living their own porno.

They were naked and had opened my wine and were licking it off each other's bare flesh. That ticked me off. I wanted to go over and demand that they reimburse me for the cost of the wine and the picnic blanket because after what they were doing on it, I was never going to touch, let alone use it again.

Before I could issue my demand for reimbursement, a real bear came out of the woods on the other side of the trail, heading right towards them

I yelled for them to watch out. They stopped writhing and

disengaged from each other.

The jogger felt around for his gun. From where I was I could see it'd slipped under some brush but he had no idea where it was. The man first looked at the bear then at the beautiful naked woman, and finally at his own feet. The guy had never taken his running shoes off.

The naked jogger stood, still unsuccessfully looking for his gun then over at the woman's feet. She'd taken off her sneakers and I could practically see the calculations for survival being run in his head. I guessed he was thinking about the old joke—he didn't have to outrun the bear, he just needed to outrun the woman. Without regard for his sex partner, he sprinted down the path and out of sight.

Now, was I disappointed that this woman had chosen the naked running guy over me? Of course I was but that didn't mean I was going to leave her alone with the bear. I dropped the bear suit then picked up a couple of long branches and lifted them over my head to make myself seem as big as possible. I heard somewhere that was what you were supposed to do when confronted with a brown bear. Supposedly, it intimidated the animals. I don't know if the bear was intimidated or not, but he did stop moving towards the blonde.

"Get behind me," I whispered.

The blonde got up slowly and moved away from the bear. I moved closer, the bear stood still. I kept moving, slowly waving my arms over my head with the branches in hopes of somehow convincing the bear that I was ten feet tall instead of five foot ten.

I risked bending down to pick up the jogger's pistol and

realized it wasn't a real gun. I recognized it from my time running track in high school—it was a starter's pistol which wouldn't exactly stop a bear.

Maybe the bear somehow knew that because it started moving towards me. I waved the remaining branch over my head but the bear wasn't impressed. As I saw things, that left me with two options. One, somehow defeat the bear in hand to paw combat. I figured I had about as much chance of doing that as I did have flying away. Which left me with my second option—scare it away.

I took the starter's pistol and fired it over my head. The sound startled the bear and it ran off.

I turned back to see the blonde, still naked, staring at me. I'll admit that I stared for a moment or two before I remembered my manners. I turned away and reached down alongside the blanket and handed over a T-shirt so she could cover up. As I held the clothes out towards her, she pulled the shirt from my hand and tossed it on the ground. Next, she grabbed me by my shirt and pulled me in for a kiss. My world exploded. In a good way. Then we made a porno of our own. I mean without cameras or anything. I guess it would have been simpler to just have said we had sex.

It was everything I dreamed it would be. We even cuddled in the afterglow, wrapped up in my picnic blanket.

"Thank you," Jogger Girl said.

I had a goofy grin and said, "It was my pleasure."

It turns out she was talking about saving her from the bear.

The beautiful lady told me to meet her there tomorrow and

to bring the gun. I didn't bother explaining it was just a starter pistol. She got dressed, gave me a kiss, and jogged off. I got dressed, picked up everything, including my bear costume and went back to my car, tossing the jogger guy's clothes in a garage can along the way.

The next day I was more than a little worried Jogger Girl wouldn't show. She did. I brought a different blanket and we went off the trail into the woods a little bit further this time and did a repeat performance with her asking me to hold the gun the entire time. During our lovemaking, she heard a noise and asked me what it was. It was a group of joggers going along the trail but I had already figured out something about being in danger turned her on. I told her it was the bear and she froze up. Then I told her not to worry, that I would protect her. Jogger Girl became much more energetic and passionate. I was worried for a bit she'd break me.

This kept up for weeks, us going at it every day from Monday to Friday but taking the weekends off because she said she had other obligations. Finally, I suggested that we go out on a real date and she laughed. Jogger Girl said we couldn't do that because her husband might find out.

That's right, my Jogger Girl was married, a rather important fact that she hadn't bothered to mention. In all fairness to me, she didn't wear a wedding ring, which I pointed out. She said she took it off when she went jogging so she didn't lose it or get mugged. I asked her if she was planning on leaving her husband for me. She very bluntly answered me that she no she wasn't. She just needed exercise to stay in shape and that sex burned almost as many calories as jogging and was far more fun. She also said what her husband didn't know wouldn't hurt him. I told her that I was looking for something more than just sex and she replied that that's all that she had to offer me. Just then, the bear showed up again, for real this time. I was so ticked off that I simply turned towards the creature and yelled for it to get out of there. Something in the tone of my voice must have been convincing because the bear ran off.

I planned to storm off but she dropped down to her knees and did several things that convinced me to stay. That happened on a Friday. I'm torn about whether or not I should meet with her on Monday. On the one hand, having sex with her almost daily has made this month the greatest of my life. On the other, I want a relationship which she's not interested in. And I don't want to be a homewrecker by breaking up somebody else's marriage. And I'm still not sure if I'll be able to talk with or meet other women. Jogger Girl doesn't actually hang around to have deep conversations. What should I do?

–Finally Getting Some In Forest Acres

Dear Some,

You must first decide which is more important to you—being in an actual romantic relationship or having regular procreation as a stranger with benefits.

There are other factors to consider. You are procreating in an area where you may eventually be spotted by others. Perhaps this is part of the thrill for one or both of you but be aware in much the same way that you snuck up upon her and man who originally owned the starter pistol and watched, others may do that to you. And since you appear to be such a fan of pornography, you should be aware that they could film your procreation and put it online without your permission. It may end up being very difficult to find out who did it and the recordings can be copied and spread by others. This risks others you both know seeing your procreational activities including Jogger Girl's husband. Her spouse may be a jealous man and prone to violence as well. Since you consistently use the same spot in the woods, if he learns of this he could follow his wife on her morning run and do great harm to one or both of you. Your starter pistol will not help you if you are put in that situation. Again you will have to decide if the benefits of regular procreation justify the risk or injury or death for you.

I recommend that you stop trying to imitate what you see in media as a way together meet or speak with human women, especially human pornography. From what Cthulhu understands, it is very unrealistic and does not work for most humans in real life. In fact, exhibiting much of that behavior can lead to assault charges being filed.

In fact, you completely misunderstood the man or bear discussion. The issue was which would women feel safer encountering alone in the woods. As the males of your species have a long history of doing bad or violent things to the females of the species without any true provocation, bears which might be able to ignore the women or be scared off much as you did is what led to so many human women saying they would choose the bear. This is despite many of the males of your species not being the kind who would harm a woman for no reason. Women have no way of knowing which type a man is based solely on outward appearance, which makes them fear for their safety when alone with an unknown human male.

In the case of your procreational partner, she feared danger from the bear and relief upon being rescued, which for her acts as an aphrodisiac. It is likely she is bored and unexcited by her continued marriage. While she will stay for the security, she craves more excitement and has found it with you at least for now.

Should you choose to continue on with the regular procreation with Jogger Girl, which is the choice most human males would go with, things may go stale. When that happens, consider leaving small amounts of food to attract the bear which, should you frighten it off rather than get eaten or mauled by it, will bring the spark back to your clandestine mating. Consider bringing bear spray just in case.

Another thing to consider. Jogger Girl is a vow breaker, willing to cheat on the spouse she pledged to be faithful to. What reason do you have to think she would be any more faithful to you and not procreate with someone who pulls her out of the way of a speeding car?

Should you choose to move on you may be surprised by an improvement in your ability to speak with the females of your species. This experience has likely given you more confidence when interacting with the opposite sex and perhaps some clue on a more typical way to start conversations.

Dear Cthulhu,

I'm one of twenty kids. My parents claimed they were going for a record until my mom had triplets and promised to cut a certain something off my dad in his sleep if he ever touched her again.

Because they only have a four-bedroom house, there were a lot of bunk and Murphy beds. My parents have some odd rules but the one that changed my life was the one that made each child move out the day after they graduated high school.

My turn was coming, but I figured out a way to buy another year by failing health class. I told them about the week before graduate that I'd failed, but they had already packed my bag. Mom went up to talk to the teacher, insisting that we knew all about human sexuality. Sadly true, as my parents had several of us sleep in their room and didn't hide what they did to make babies. The teacher relented and passed me.

So I graduated. I hadn't applied to colleges because another rule of the house was nobody's college was paid for. If we wanted to go, it was up to each of us to cover tuition. I wasn't an athlete or a brain so I wasn't going to get any scholarships, so what was the point of applying?

The next day at noon my parents walked me to the end of the driveway. Dad shook my hand and mom gave me a hug, then handed me a lunch she made. Then they told me they didn't want to see me until Thanksgiving.

I had nowhere to go so I slept at the bus station. I saw the flyer that changed my life. It advertised truck driving jobs and the place doing the hiring was only a few miles away. I didn't have a driver's license let alone the CDL that you needed to drive a truck. My parents said it would be too exhausting to teach all of us to drive so they didn't teach any of us. Yet another house rule.

The one thing I did excel at in high school was partying. In pursuit of that skill set I got a fake id made by an artist friend of mine. As luck would have it, it was a CDL.

I put my bag in a locker, washed up in the men's room and walked two miles to the trucking office. The interview went great and since I already had the license, they hired me on the spot.

They put me in a truck, gave me a GPS, and told me where to drive to. I'll admit I ground a few gears and almost jackknifed three times but by the time I got there, I had it down. That night, I watched a bunch of MeTube videos to learn more and within a few weeks I was more than competent.

The problem is my fake ID "expired" in two years and that time is up. I can't renew it because it's not real. I can't get another because my artist buddy died after trying to scare a guy on a foot bridge while wearing, oddly enough, a mask of you, Cthulhu. The guy freaked and threw him off the bridge. He hit his head on a rock and drowned. He had a buddy recording the whole thing for his Klik Klok channel. The buddy posted it anyway and it went viral.

What am I going to do? Once my bosses find out I don't have a license, they'll fire me. I've worked very hard all these years and never got so much as a ticket. I just can't figure out how to get out of this which stinks because I love my job. I'm afraid that if I go to the DMV, I'll be found out, and maybe end up arrested or at least fined. I've been sleeping in the bed of my truck and spending what I would spend on rent on partying, so I'll be homeless again. And since I'm not twenty one yet, my partying will be on hold for almost a year.

What should I do?

–Real Truck Driver With A Fake License in Redding

Dear Fake,

You have a few options available. One would be to try to find someone of equal skill to provide you with a new fake ID, but this only delays the problem and allows the potential for much more harm. I can understand your reluctance to go to the DMV.

First get a permit and then take a test to get a regular driver's license. That will allow you to sign up for classes to get your CDL. In your state it takes four weeks to train and two more weeks to receive your license. If you have enough time before your fake ID expires, sign up and take the class and pass.

If not, do not worry yet. True, your employer will be upset and try to fire you, but do not sign anything. Point out to them if they fire you, it would come out that for almost two years they had employed someone who not only didn't have a CDL but didn't have any sort of driver's license. Not only would it reflect poorly on them, it would likely result in a staggering amount of fines for their company. Perhaps someone in the company is an instructor and would be willing to sign off that you already have the required hours to take the test. In less than two months, this problem is solved. In case your employer later retaliates over these threats, consider at least renting a room somewhere so you do not end up homeless.

Dear Cthulhu,

They've been trying to build a new hotel in my town for a few years now. They got some of the framework and walls up before they ran out of funding and ran into a permit issue. Mainly, I think they forgot to bribe the building inspector and he shut them down. About that time, my girlfriend broke up with me and kicked me out because I cheated on her with her houseplant. I tried explaining that I was drunk and the ficus didn't mean anything to me, but the video that I posted on Instaface went viral so she wasn't having any of it.

I didn't have a job and had pretty much been sponging off her after my parents cut me off after they caught me in the garden with a fern.

I needed a place to stay and, after my viral experience, none of my friends or relations wanted me in their house because they feared for the safety of their plants. I wandered around town and when I got to the half–built hotel, I snuck inside and spent the night. Over the next week, I hit some church outreach groups. They gave me a sleeping bag and some clothes, and even told me where I could eat for free. Between the three places, I get four meals a day, which is more than I got from my girlfriend. Or my parents. Plus, I don't have to cook any of it. Not that I was a great cook, but it's a pain in the neck to take those frozen dinners out of the box, remember to put a hole in the cellophane then wait 5 to 8 minutes until it's done cooking.

One of the shelters even has a shower so I don't even stink. Plus, a nearby business got rid of their office plants, so I took them back to the hotel with me, so I haven't even been lonely.

I go to people's recycling bins and take the newspapers and magazines, so I have something to read, but I'm always about a week behind on the news and current events. I recently read an article that said the funding to finish the hotel had been acquired and that the building permits were in place.

That means construction crews will be coming to finish the hotel. They are bound to notice me squatting here and kick me out. They might even take away my new plant friends.

What can I do? Do I have any legal recourse? Can I get somebody to sue them so they can't kick me out? Or maybe force them to give me a permanent room in the hotel when it's finished. It'd be nice to have TV again. Or should I chain myself to the support beams and refuse to leave? Don't squatters have rights?

Help me Cthulhu, so I don't have to lose my home, or worse, have to get a job.

–Squatter In A Hotel With No Room Service In Syracuse

Dear Squatter,

As you are squatting at a commercial property, I'm not sure you would have traditional squatter's rights. To find out, you would need to hire an attorney, which means you would need money to pay for their time, something it sounds like you do not have. As for chaining yourself to the support beams, it may be your best option. Not that it's a good one and likely will only slow your being kicked out. Perhaps you will get beaten and be able to get a lawyer to sue on your behalf, taking a contingency fee.

You might be able to get some small amount of social media coverage of your plight. Especially if you arrange for someone to film and post it with a sob story about how the hotel is picking on someone who is poor and displaced, but only if you get enough views and somebody cares. Most probably won't. Now, if you were a dog or hedgehog, it might be a different story. At best, they might hand you a few bucks to go away, but you will be lucky to get a coupon for half off your next stay at their hotel.

Dear Cthulhu,

I was born with powers and abilities far beyond those of normal people. I have what is possibly the most useful superpower ever. When I'm stuck at a red light, I can think about it and make the light turn green. This power makes my life easier and lessens the amount of time I spend stuck in traffic. The problem is none of my friends believe me so, to prove it, I took them all out for a ride to demonstrate my abilities. They all said that I just waited until near the end of the traffic light cycle and that I wasn't changing the light. Then they had the nerve to claim that I just had the timing down so when I yelled the word "change" it looked like I was doing it, which is ridiculous. Changing electrical patterns is not an easy task and has to be done just right. Otherwise, it will short out and destroy the system. I have no desire to cause my town to have to replace all those traffic lights just because I was in a little bit of a hurry.

How do I change the opinions of my disbelieving friends?

–Game–Changing Light Changer In Chattanooga

Dear Light,

From your description, it is highly unlikely that you possess the power you claim, which means your friends are probably right. You get bored when you sit at a traffic light. Because you want to go, you think about it. Then when it happens you believe you caused it, when in reality you had no effect on the time it took the light to cycle from red to green. And in most places, lights are not very long so you could give yourself the delusional perception that you're causing the change.

There is an infinitesimal chance that you are one of the few humans who possess some sort of psychic ability. Despite claims made to the contrary, that sort of talent is almost non–existent in your population. The best way to find out for sure is to test it under controlled circumstances. Many universities still get grants from the government to test for the existence of powers similar to yours so they can be used to further the government's aims in espionage. You could simply volunteer for the studies at the end of which, you will likely be told you have no abilities. However, if you are visited by men and women in dark suits in the middle of the night who then take you far away from your disbelieving friends for a new government job, congratulations, you were right.

If you cannot get into such a program, Cthulhu will test you. If do indeed have powers, Cthulhu will allow you to use them for his benefit. If not, you become that week's sacrifice and souffle for my worship service.

Dear Cthulhu,

I am absolutely devastated about what you did for me. Or rather what you didn't do.

I was very happy as a recent convert to the Cult of Cthulhu. The welcome basket was lovely and the religious philosophy of putting yourself ahead of all others except for Great Cthulhu aligned very nicely with my personal views. My favorite part of the religion was that you let your worshipers put names in a hat for people they'd like to see be the next human sacrifice. Sure it's a lottery for whoever gets picked, but just the idea that my lousy boss at work, my former best friend who slept with my ex-boyfriend, or that smoking hot barista at Spacebucks who refused to have sex with me in the bathroom because he didn't "find me attractive" getting tied down on your altar and screaming and writhing in pain as they are sacrificed to your greater glory is often enough to take an otherwise gloomy day and turn my frown upside down.

One of the other reasons I joined was that in all the other religions I tried out, the deities being worshiped never showed up at service, whether to get their belly rubbed for luck, shake the worshippers' hands, or turn some water into Sangria. In your temple, we actually got to see you. Not in person since our temple is relatively small but you did have a room for video chats so we could see proof of your great and terrible existence.

Because of that, I expected so much more from you. Frankly, Great Cthulhu, you let me down in a big way. I was out at the bar and picked up a guy around last call who said he was willing to be my love slave. No one else had ever offered before, so I wasn't about to turn him down. We got in my car so I could take him home but he was revved up higher than my engine and leaned over to put his head in my lap while I was driving.

Okay, maybe I was taking the whole love slave thing a little too serious and perhaps I grabbed his hair and pushed him down. Still, he didn't complain and began making me a very happy woman. What I wasn't expecting was for him to be so skilled that he'd make me happier than anyone else ever had. I couldn't control myself and ended up throwing my head back, closing my eyes, and screaming in ecstasy.

In hindsight, it was a bad idea to take my eyes off the road. I still have no idea where the llama came from.

It collided with my bumper, then my hood and then kept coming through my windshield. At least its head did. Staring into that animal's eyes wasn't some beautiful life changing experience. Not for me anyway. The thing screamed at me. I screamed back and tried to swerve away, but the head was wedged through the cracked glass and not going anywhere. My car lost control and spun out. I struggled with the wheel, hit the break then the gas but the car wouldn't slow down or go where I wanted it to.

Instead of trying more of the same thing and expecting a different result – the very different definition of crazy – I threw my hands up in the air and yelled, "Cthulhu take the wheel!"

Well, did you? You already know the answer. You did not. Instead of slowing down and steering itself to safety, my car went over an embankment, flipping over and over until it crashed at the bottom, landing upside-down.

I'll have you know that my face got smashed up by the

airbag and I got a long purple bruise along where the seatbelt held me in place. As horrible as that is, it didn't even compare to what happened to my love slave who didn't have his seatbelt on. The airbag snapped his neck, killing him instantly. It also rammed the llama's neck against the jagged aid edges of my broken windshield and decapitated the horrid beast.

Worst of all, I didn't get to go home and bang my love slave. I mean, I suppose there might have been some way to sneak his corpse into my house but where would the fun in that be? He wasn't as hot as the barista but if the skills that man showed me were indicative of what he could do, I would have had the best night of my life.

Instead, I got to lay upside down in a crushed car for an hour and a half until the fire department cut me out with the jaws of life. I spent all that time staring into the upside-down eyes of the decapitated llama. I suppose it was lucky it took so long because I was able to move my love slave over so his head wasn't in my lap, as that would have been hard to explain.

And explain I had to. When a lot of people have accidents, they blame it on animals that weren't there, but it was pretty hard for the police to dispute my story about a llama since there was one in two pieces at the crash site. And just when I thought things couldn't get any worse, they made me even more embarrassed by asking me my passenger's name. I didn't know it because we haven't bothered with introductions. We had more important matters to attend to than getting to know each other.

Plus, even though I moved him out of my lap he was still pinned in an unusual position, which made the police and firefighters speculate about what might have been happening right before the crash. I denied it of course but I'm not sure if they believed me.

Because of your inaction, I have a wrecked car and bruises on the upper half of my body. I am the only thing the gossipy busybodies in town are talking about, and, worst of all, I missed out on what would have probably been the best sex of my life. What were you doing that was so important that you couldn't come to the aid of one of your worshipers?

– Abandoned Worshiper Of Someone Who Couldn't Be Bothered

Dear Abandoned,

The sheer audacity and vapidity of you having penned this letter, let alone sending it is staggering. This is what happens when one gets rid of the IQ test for new worshipers. It increased the numbers of my cult but greatly decreased the quality.

I imagine the doctors who looked at you in the emergency room weren't very thorough because you appear to have suffered a traumatic brain injury. Why else would you dare address me in this way? Cthulhu shall address the consequences of your poor manners momentarily.

First, why do you and so many other humans assume just because you pray to the object of your worship for something that you will automatically receive it? While Cthulhu answers all requests from his worshipers, most of the time Cthulhu's answer is no.

Back to your case. What makes you think that Cthulhu did not come to your aid? How else do you think you survived that accident if not for Cthulhu's intervention?

Instead of groveling and singing your everlasting thanks to Cthulhu, you accuse me in a disrespectful, uncouth, and rude manner. Having had the privilege of sitting through the Dark Scriptures of Cthulhu classes, my worshippers – yourself included – know there are consequences for their actions. Your actions resulted in damage to the property of Cthulhu.

When you became a member of my cult, you signed over everything that is yours – mind, body, soul, and worldly possessions – to Cthulhu and this is how you take care of what belongs to me?

There is a silver lining in all this. Your little temple will be getting a personal visit from great Cthulhu this week regarding the winner of this month's human sacrifice lottery. Instead of ritually slaying a random contestant suggested by my worshippers, you will be the sacrifice. And we will start by cutting off the fingers you used to type those words and then dust off the breaking wheel from Cthulhu's collection of implements of torture. Do not look it up on the internet. It would be unfortunate if you died of fright before sacrifice night.

Cthulhu looks forward to seeing you again very soon.

Dear Cthulhu,

I have a daughter who's driving me crazy. She used to be a wonderful child, as sweet as can be. Ever since she turned 13, she has done nothing but yell and scream at everybody and tell us what horrible parents we are. I work sixty hours a week so I don't have much time at home. I was used to having quality time with my kid when I came home, not this teenaged battlefield.

My wife goes to church a lot and thinks my daughter is possessed. She even wants our daughter to have an exorcism, but the minister at the church won't do it unless both parents sign off. It seems members of other churches have killed children in the past who just had epilepsy or things like that so the form is a necessity.

I was homeschooled and only had brothers, so I'm not really sure what the best way to raise a daughter is. Despite that, it doesn't seem to me that exorcism is the right way to go. What do you think I should do?

–Dad At The End Of His Line In Lafayette

Dear Lafayette,

Cthulhu highly doubts that your daughter is possessed. What is most likely happening is she has hit puberty and hormones are raging through her and making her act the way you describe. It is not uncommon for human females to become loud, argumentative, and angry during this change in life. It can happen to males as well, but the females of your species seem to have gotten it worse. What your daughter needs is for you to remain as calm as possible, give her space, and from what Cthulhu's letters have told me, provide her with lots of chocolate. On the plus side, in five to ten years she should be out living on her own so you only have to do your best to hold on until then. I've had naps that lasted longer than that.

Dear Cthulhu,

I recently saw the letter in your column from the man who felt he was born in the wrong time and body because he knew he was really a Viking. I'm in a similar predicament. I know in reality that I should be a racecar driver, yet none of the professional racing organizations will hire me or give me a car. Since I know I'm really a racecar driver, can I sue them for denying me my innate rights?

–Fast Eddie In Edwardstown

Dear Fast,

Cthulhu is not sure where humans have gotten the idea that just because they want something, the world is obligated to give it to them. Except in Cthulhu's case, life doesn't work this way. No one is going to just suddenly come along and wave a magic wand to make you into a racecar driver. Win or lose, a lawsuit will not suddenly grant you a new skill set.

What you need to do is research what goes into making someone a racecar driver and then work along that path so you can achieve your goal. Have you ever driven a car on a racetrack? You may work hard to get the chance to try out to be a racecar driver and then find you do not have the aptitude. If you cannot handle driving a car at a rapid pace in counterclockwise circles without hitting other cars or walls, then it seems a foolish career choice. If you have the natural talent and work hard enough to develop your skills, you might get a shot but getting that chance is no guarantee of success.

Another option is available if you do not want to work hard or do not have the talent. There are places that do have fantasy driving, where for a sum of money they will let you drive an actual racecar on a real track to give you the feeling of what it would be like to be a racecar driver. If you have the means, this may be the most practical option for you.

Your final option is join the world of outlaw racing, glamorized in *The Quick and The Curious* movies. There you will develop the skills you need to race or die in the process. Either way, your problem is solved.

Dear Cthulhu,

I'm not a very manly–looking fellow. I'm only five–two and clock in out about ninety–eight pounds if I just ate. As skinny as I am, my face is also topped off with what some would describe as delicate features. Despite working out up to five days a week, I've never been able to bulk up. Even with a crew cut, I'm constantly being mistaken for a teenage girl. I'm a guy in my late twenties. It's embarrassing.

I did the only thing I could think of to change my appearance. I grew a beard. Turns out, growing a beard is something I'm good at. It came in thick and luxurious. Growing facial hair may be the only thing I'm good at. I got laid off from my job about six months ago and I've run through all my savings. I'm at the point where I may have to move back in with my parents.

Here's the odd thing — even with the facial hair, I still look like a teenage girl. I went to the carnival and they offered me a job as their bearded lady. At first, I was insulted. Then they told me what it paid plus a percentage of the take for customers paying to see me and any merchandizing. It's significantly more than I was making in my factory job. We'd be on the road so my friends and family wouldn't see me. When we played my hometown, I could opt out. I wouldn't even need to use my real name as they insist my stage name be female for obvious reasons as nobody would pay to see Zeke the bearded lady.

I was raised religious, so it feels a bit wrong to not be telling the truth, but it also seems way wrong to have to move back in with my parents at almost thirty. Plus, the merboy and the chicken lady aren't what they really claim to be. The carnival owner says the people come to see the sideshow because, at least on some level, they want to be fooled.

I can move my stuff into my parents' garage and the carnival gives me a place to sleep so I won't have any rent and they'll feed me. I figure if I do it for two or three years, I'd have enough to put at least half the money down on a house in my hometown and get a more typical job if I want to.

Would it be wrong for me to deceive people this way?

–Bearded Dude Who Looks Like A Lady In Lake Marie

Dear Bearded,

The carnival owner is correct. Few humans expect carnival sideshows to be 100% legitimate. Sure, there are people with natural differences that are real, but those are usually at the bigger shows. Many of the traveling shows manufacture their acts, so you will be following a long tradition. If this is something you feel you can do, you're not hurting anyone and in fact, you might be giving people something to talk about as they pity the young girl with the thick facial hair.

Cthulhu also has a suggestion for when you retire from the carnival to help you be perceived as your biological gender. In your society, very few women shave their heads without a medical reason. Try shaving yours but leave either a beard or a goatee. That combination may be enough to convince people that you are a man.

Dear Cthulhu,

I've never had much luck with the opposite sex. Women just never seem to find me attractive. I've never had a second date and I haven't had many first dates.

That all changed when I met "Tess" in a "Lobsters Are Pets Not Food" chat room. We had so many of the same interests that we just clicked. It was like we'd known each other forever. We chatted and texted, then started talking on the phone. After six months of talking every night, we finally decided we were going to meet at a bar. Even the meeting place was a thrill for us both. Neither one of us had ever been picked up in a bar before and we both wanted to scratch it off our bucket lists.

To be honest, I was a little nervous that I was being catfished. Tess sounded like a woman, but she always refused to video chat with me, which made me a little suspicious. She could've really been a man who really hated the idea of keeping lobsters as pets and ate them instead. Either would've been a deal breaker.

I got to the bar early and ordered myself a martini, shaken not stirred. Not that I knew a lot about drinking but I'd seen that in the movies enough times to know how to order it.

There was a guy at the bar sitting next to me with a line of three empty beer mugs in front of him. I figured he was there for the same reason I was, to meet some girl that he'd been chatting with online. We got to talking. He'd been waiting over an hour for a girl he'd met on the Humper app and she hadn't shown up. She told him to wear a red carnation in his collar, which looked silly in his *Chainsaw Nightmares VI: Buzzkill, Clown In The Dark* movie t-shirt. The guy was fed up waiting, took the carnation out, and handed it to me. He told me maybe I'd have better luck with it than he did then split.

Ten minutes later, Tess walked in and saw me sitting at the bar and strutted over. I'd sent her a real picture of me but apparently she hadn't done the same. It must have been a test because in her picture she was kind of plain and dumpy, but in real life she was smoking hot.

I was still holding the red carnation. She said, "Nice flower." Then she straddled me right on my bar stool and kissed me like I'd never been kissed before. Which was literally the easiest thing ever since I hadn't. When we came up for air, she said it was nice to meet me and why didn't we blow this popsicle stand.

I told her I'd rented a motel room nearby. She said she couldn't wait that long and dragged me into the backseat of my car and made me a man. It was amazing. Then we went back to the motel room and she made me a whole bunch of men. It seems I have a very good recovery time. I mean I should. My equipment was basically brand–new and had never been used before. After she made me a man for the fourth time, we passed out in bed together. I fall asleep dreaming of our wedding. She was gorgeous and our chemistry together was incredible, the stuff romantic Christmas movies were made of.

In the morning, I woke to answer nature's call and saw my phone was blinking and brought it into the bathroom with me. Tess was blowing up my phone, leaving me a dozen texts which was impressive since I'd never seen her even touch her phone. As I was in the middle of my answer to nature's call, another text came in. I didn't bother to read it and just texted her back one-handed, saying how sweet it was for her to text me from the next room and did she miss me already?

The next text was in all caps with her yelling at me, demanding to know what the hell I was talking about. I scrolled back through her texts. It seemed she had had car trouble in a dead zone and couldn't call me to tell me she was going to get to the bar late. She demanded to know where I was and who I was with.

I was a bit curious about that part myself. I finished taking care of nature's call and peeked out the door. The woman who I spent the night with was still curled up asleep in bed, her phone untouched.

Tess was texting that I'd cheated on her.

I cursed then woke up the woman who had manned me up four times. I demanded to know why she impersonated Tess and who did she think she was to take advantage of me like that.

She smiled and climbed out of bed naked, then took my phone out of my hand and tossed it across the room. Then she made me forget about my questions in a strive for five.

I had prepared a cold feast for Tess and stuck it in the room's fridge before I went to the bar. It seemed a shame to waste it, so I served the naked lady breakfast. All lobster free, of course.

She explained to me that she found that her husband cheated on her with her sister so she was using dating apps like Humper and DoMeNow to sleep with a different man every night. Because I'd been holding the red carnation, last night had been my turn. She had run late because she slept with her Zuber driver instead of paying him. The guy at the bar had just given up too soon. His loss was my gain.

When she told me that our time together was done and we'd never see each other again, my visions of us getting married vanished. I asked her if she'd be willing to leave her husband for me. She asked if I was rich. When I said no, she said I was good but not that good.

I smiled and blushed because she said I was good. It was my first "times" out after all. I suggested that I could be her regular Wednesday night guy. She laughed and said I was cute, then kissed me. That led to our last time together.

She didn't leave a number or email, or even her name. Fake Tess hadn't objected to me calling her Tess earlier. I watched her climb into the front seat of a Zuber and her head disappeared from sight as the car drove away.

I haven't seen her since.

I went back into my motel room and read all the real Tess's even more angry texts and more accusations of me cheating on her. I countered that I wasn't cheating because I thought it was her. I didn't mention the fifth and sixth times when I knew she wasn't Tess because I'm not stupid.

Cthulhu, do you think I cheated? Technically we'd never met in person so she can't claim we had an actual relationship, let alone an exclusive one.

To be honest, any relationship we had was based more on desperation because no one else would have anything to do with us rather than an unstated exclusivity. I still think Tess and I clicked well together and now that I've actually had sex, I want to keep having it. I've been trying to get her to meet me for real but she says she's too mad. I'd really like to see if we can make this relationship work. What should I do?

–Accidental Stud In Albuquerque

Dear Accidental,

If no vows were stated, none could be broken. Since no exclusive arrangement was made, you have not cheated on her by procreating with someone who wasn't her. Your argument that it should not count because you thought it was her may seem logical to you, but will not hold water with most of the females of your species even if it is true.

Whether or not it would be worth your while to attempt to advance this relationship is another matter. You still do not know if this Tess is a woman. You do not know her age, what she looks like, or anything about her physically. You do not know if anything you have discussed is true or not. It has been Cthulhu's experience that even desperate humans place value on looks, although emotions can make someone who might be generally considered less physically attractive appear to be the most beautiful person to someone infatuated with them. Alcohol can do the same thing. Both have aided in the continued propagation of your species.

Be honest with Tess and tell her the only reason you slept with this other woman is because you thought it was her. State that you would like to make it up to her but the only way you can is if she agrees to meet you. Then you can determine if she is indeed a woman that you do find attractive and would like to procreate with. You may end up meeting her and decide a relationship is not something you want. Or you could find the human you want to spend the rest of your life with. More likely, it will end up being something in between.

Dear Cthulhu,

I hate the government. It's constantly sticking its nose where it need not be. I don't want to pay taxes but I do it so that them bureaucrats in Washington leave me the blazes alone. The problem is that ain't enough for them blood sucking government folks.

I'm sure you remember that fake plague that shut down the world a while back. My wife begged me to get the jab, but I didn't, even though my cousin supposedly died from the fake plague. I wasn't gonna get the ouchi and let them put a microchip inside of me, no siree. Live free or die I say, although my wife pointed out that if the plague wasn't fake that I might be able to do both.

Despite my best efforts, I've been vaccinated against my will. A few months back, I fell off a ladder at work while doing some demolition and impaled my leg on some rusty rebar. I also smashed my skull on a block of concrete so I was unconscious when the ambulance brought me to the hospital. They operated on me and got the rebar out. It had stabbed all the way through my leg. Since I was in Lala land from my noggin bump and the happy juice they used during the surgery, these shifty doctors asked my wife if they could give me a tetanus shot. Notice how they call it a shot, like it's something good like whiskey? They don't call it no jab or vaccine because they think we're too stupid to know any better. Unfortunately, my wife *was* too stupid to know better and told them that they could stab me with their damnable vaccine needle.

When I came out, I laid into that woman because she knew I didn't want none of that doctor voodoo in my body but she let them do it. She said that they told her that my jaw could lock up, be in terrible pain and get seizures. I told her that woulda been better than having the government microchip in my body. I may have called her some unkind words. My so-called wife replied with some unkind words of her own. That woman had the gall to tell me that she regretted letting me get the shot because if my jaw locked up I wouldn't be able to talk and that would be a pleasure for her. I replied that maybe I should jab and stab her with a rusty pipe so her jaw froze and she'd finally quit yapping at me. She was not pleased with the way I defended my God-given rights to control what goes into my body and the long and short of it is she left me to move back in with her nasty ole mama.

I demanded the hospital fix what they did to me by draining all the microchip-tainted blood out of me and replacing it with the unvaccinated variety like from the babies in the maternity ward. They said the babies needed their blood. I told them I needed it more and they could just give my old blood to the rug rats. They said doing that would put the babies' lives in danger. I countered by saying that the world is a dangerous place and the quicker these freeloading babies learn that, the better off they'll be. Besides a grown man's well-being has got to be worth that of a few babies just by body weight alone. Apparently babies only got a half-pint of blood and a full-grown person's got like eight or twelve so it would take up to twenty-four babies to fill up my tank. I said then we better get started and if they didn't have enough tots in stock, they better get on the horn to the other hospitals to get more. They refused and put a police guard on my door and said I wasn't allowed to leave my room until I left the hospital.

But that only proved my point cause the police are part of the government which meant the dang government was trying to keep a patriotic man down.

I wasn't about to become the government's plaything so I lined the inside of my house with thick foil I found on the internet to make sure signals from the microchip in me can't reach those government 5G information collectors in the cell phone towers. I also lined my car with the same foil so they can't track me. Well, technically they told me I shouldn't drive with my beat up leg for at least two months, but they also said there was no microchip in my jab, so why would I listen to doctors who lie?

The only problem is the foil is blocking my cell phone signal and I can't watch my pornography or play Kandy Smush or Poka-a-guy Go.

I tried to make a suit out of the foil so I could walk around without the government tracking me and still use my phone for necessities but it's not a very flexible material. Every time I walk or move my arms it cracks or tears. And when I sit down, it breaks in half.

I figure if I can learn a few things, I can get my life back to normal so can you tell me where the microchips from the vaccinations usually end up settling in the human body? My buddy says in the heart so if we stand up against the government it can give us a shocking to kill us but I kind of figured it would jam itself up behind the eye so the government could see everything we do. I was thinking that if I knew where the chip was, I could just put foil over that body part and call it a day. Or do you by chance know of anywhere I can get a suit that would block the microchip signal? I could wear it on my social outings since my traitorous wife done run off on me which means I'm back on the market. It's been my experience that women tend to look at a fellow wearing metal foil as clothing body as a little wacky do, which obviously I am not, and I want to play on feminine sympathy about my leg injury. The story I'm telling is I was defending my home from a bunch of woke liberal transpecies commies who wanted to take away my guns and chainsaws. There were twenty of them trying to crucify me but I fought them off despite them having got a quarter of the crucifying done. They had picked on the wrong patriot. I figure I'm gonna have to beat the chicks off with a stick with that story.

–Microchipped in Murfreesboro

Dear Microchipped,

There may indeed end up being some beating with a stick though not in the way you are thinking.

You are going through a lot of trouble no reason. Assuming such nanotechnology existed and could be mass–produced, its cost would be prohibitive and if there is one thing governments hate to do is to spend money that doesn't line their pockets or help them be reelected.

The resources needed to microchip everyone is more than your government is able to commit to the task when they can hack into people's smart phone instead to read your messages, check your browsing history, and your location. Cthulhu has heard the arguments that you can turn off your location, but that is only a limited truth as the phone itself is still connecting with cell phone towers and can still be tracked. It just denies your location to certain apps.

Not that they don't microchip some people but those humans typically are spies or committing major crimes, terrorist acts, or not paying their taxes. Best to try to blend in and hope they will not notice your existence.

As to the idea that a microchip could be used to kill you, Cthulhu points out that a microchip with that capacity would cost a great deal of money and they have much more inexpensive ways of killing people such as using a bullet or some poison, which would likely cost your government less than a dollar.

However when Cthulhu's scientists perfect the mind control microchip or make water addictive, that will change.

Dear Cthulhu,

I recently read the letter you answered from a fellow truck driver so I decided to write you as well. I have a different issue. Like *Real Truck Driver With A Phony License in Redding*, I love my job and the open road. I enjoy spending time by myself listening to the radio. Driving a truck gives me a way to earn money while doing both those things. Plus, I help provide the citizens of this great nation with the things they need by moving them throughout this beautiful land. I've always arranged my schedule so that I have a few days to hang out and have fun wherever I drop off a load. It's allowed me to meet and become friends with a lot of wonderful people, my three husbands in particular.

Despite how it sounds, I'm not a bigamist. The men just think we're married. What I did in each case was have a friend of mine in each city pretend to be a justice of the peace and perform the ceremony. I also found a couple of strangers to sign a fake name on a phony document, saying they witnessed the blessed nuptials. I feed each of the guys a line about how I'm not into big crowds after making up some cock and bull story about how our wedding is our day and that we shouldn't have to share something so special with anybody else.

It's worked four times so far.

Yes, I did have a fourth "husband," but a while ago I just drove away from him and never went back. It was fully justified, mind you. I came home after not having visited him for a few months and he greeted me at the door with another woman. Then he said he wanted a threesome. I have no interest in ladies, so who was this woman for? Not me, that's for sure. The one thing I'm honest about with each of my fake husbands is that I demand loyalty and total fidelity. And if I let him have his fun even once, that would be opening the door to him sleeping with her again when I'm not around, which is most of the time.

My answer was short and sweet. I went to my truck cab and got the tire iron I keep under my seat for when I have trouble on the road with morons who think I'm a helpless female. They learn different when I knock them upside the head with some grade–A American steel. I planned to do the same to this homewrecking whore, but she was too fast and took off down the street in see–through lingerie and 6–inch stiletto heels. I had to give her credit—she was track star fast on those mini–stilts and got away.

Next, I turned to number four who dropped to his knees to beg my forgiveness and for me not to bash his brains in.

As long as he was down there, I put him to work servicing my needs until he satisfied me three times and then passed out without returning the favor. He didn't press the issue since I never let go of the tire iron.

I abhor liars and cheaters, so I left the would-be adulterer in the middle of the night and never went back. He hasn't been able to find me as I keep off all social media and deactivated the cell phone that I used to talk with him. Plus, I had given him a phony name.

Truth be told, I have the perfect life. I have three perfect husbands, at least perfect enough to make 2 to 3 days at a time seem like heaven. I tell you, Mormons have the right idea. Except that they only let the guys do it.

If I ever decide I no longer like any of these men, I'll take off like I did with number four and never go back. I keep the only copies of the fake marriage licenses and we rarely socialize with other people because I just complain that I'm tired from all the driving I do and tell them I just want to spend all my time with them.

Now something threatens to unravel and destroy my entire way of life.

My employer decided to have a bring your spouse to work week. I'm careful to make sure I keep the different aspects of my life apart from each other, which is one of the reasons I stay off social media and give the men fake names. I also use a PO Box as my address. When I'm not with the hubby of the day, I sack out in the sleeper bed of my truck. The problem is my husbands have all seen the logo on the side of my truck, so they know who I work for, even if they don't know my real name. Number Four even tried to find me through them but they had no record of the name I gave him and he doesn't have the money to hire a PI to find me.

It turns out that the other three all check the company website periodically so they found out about the event.

There is no freaking way I can bring all three of them with me in my rig for a week. For one, it'd be hard to hide the fact that there are two other guys there. It wouldn't be long before they talked to each other and figured things out. Two, it's against regulations to have that many people in the cab at once and I don't want to get written up.

Yes, I could take my favorite for that week and just walk out on the other two. The problem is then I'd have to find more men to replace them. Believe it or not, it's hard to get dudes to buy into my story and go along with the situation, especially since I make each of them cover their own rent and bills. I explain to them that I give most of my money to charity to help support the poor clowns who are homeless and jobless because the circus had to shut down.

I make too much money and have too much seniority to quit my job and find another one. I'm up to four weeks' vacation. If I quit, I'd have to go back down to two weeks at a new job plus take a cut in pay. I usually use at least one of those vacation weeks to take a singles' cruise.

I'm trying to figure out exactly how I'm going to make this work. I know if anyone could help me, it would be you Cthulhu.

–True Blue Trucker With Three Phony Husbands

Dear Phony,

Your predicament, like that of most humans, is of your own doing. The men who think they are married to you are being misled but they must have some idea that something is off with these sham marriages. Yet for some reason, they remain pretend-married to you, which means you're filling some sort of need for them. Although I suspect their opinions might change if they had confirmation of what you were doing.

One option is to come clean and see if any of them are okay with the situation. However, that outcome is unlikely. A better solution would simply be to make up some phony excuse for two of them about why that week would not work and take one the week before, one the week of, and the last the week after which should work to avoid them having to cross paths.

As it sounds like you've never spent more than three days with any of your fake husbands, the full week might be a bonding experience for you as couples. Or it might serve to enlighten them as to your true character. Either way, it is your best option because if you deny them this, they will be upset and they will start looking for the reasons why you left them at home. It will most likely not end well for you.

If you get involved in any future sham marriages, you might want to consider investing in a few large magnetic signs for the side of your truck. You can put your fake name down on the sign and stick it over the real logo. That way any newcomers won't be checking your company website which would help you avoid this happening again. You could even try it on the present fake husbands and tell them that you went into business for yourself. And if any look underneath, you can say you bought the truck from your former employer and did not have the cash to have it painted. And avoid future problems like company picnics and holiday parties.

Dear Cthulhu,

I'm a 12-year-old girl with very limited employment opportunities. Plain and simple, it's age discrimination. I can't even legally get a job until I turn 16, so how am I supposed to afford my cell phone, Polka-a-guy cards, and video games? Let alone the occasional visit to Maury Mozzarella's.

My dad made a suggestion—I could use his lawnmower to mow the yards of our neighbors in exchange for money. It was a great idea. I got ten houses in our neighborhood to pay me to mow their lawns every week. I was rolling in dough.

The only problem is I gave my dad a bill for mowing his lawn. I should point out that I was given mowing our lawn as part of my chores last year and I have been doing it ever since. I figure if the neighbors are willing to pay me for my services, my dad should too.

And I told him that. You know what he told me? That mowing the lawn was part of my responsibilities for living in our house.

I told him tough, if he wanted me to mow the lawn, he was going to have to pay me. I figured my dad had caved to my superior negotiating skills when he chuckled and said sure. Then he sat down and wrote stuff on a piece of paper and handed it to me. My dad had made a bill and wanted to charge me a rental fee for using the lawnmower that came to twice what I was charging him to mow the lawn. He even added in the gas he had to buy for me to use in the mower when I did the neighbors' lawns.

I told him fine, I'd use the money I saved up and buy my own lawnmower. You know what he did? He handed me another bill. This one had rent, food, clothes, and even a fee to use the Wi-Fi. He said he was going to make me pay for my cell phone. (I may have been exaggerating earlier when I implied that I paid for my own cell phone service.) It's five times what I earn every week mowing lawns and he said I would have to pay it all year long. Mowing lawns is a seasonal business. It's not like I can do it in the wintertime.

How can I make my father be more reasonable and drop all the stupid billing of me and just pay me for my work?

–Trying To Mow The Man Down In Montana

Dear Mow,

While Cthulhu admires your entrepreneurial spirit, there are many humans, especially young ones, who expect other people to take care of them entirely. You proved with your whining that you buy into that as well, at least where your father is concerned. In this world, no one owes you anything. However, in many cases, parents are willing to give to their children because they love them or feel responsible or guilty for bringing them onto this mismanaged planet. It is rather incomprehensible to me.

Your father was letting you use the lawnmower out of some sort of misguided parental love, trying to teach you how to get along in life. The only fee he was charging you was mowing the lawn of the home you live in, which you had been doing anyway. He tried to make a point by charging you double what you wanted to charge him, but you were too dense or dumb to understand the point he was trying to make. If you had simply agreed to continue mowing your lawn for free, I suspect your father would've dropped his charges. When you tried to outsmart him by threatening to buy your own mower, he simply upped his game in hopes that his new demands would prove his point.

You said it yourself, at 12 years old you are unable to make a living for yourself so you cannot leave your father's home to go live on your own. Swallow your misguided ego, apologize, and mow the lawn. Think of it as overhead costs that you are paying in labor. Or take the money you have earned and buy a tent and see how you enjoy living in it and being homeless. I suspect you'll see the wisdom of doing what your father asked.

Also, you're missing out on another source of income. In the wintertime, where you live there is snow. You can approach the same customers whom you mow lawns for and offer to shovel their walks and driveways for a fee. Or if your father has a snowblower, you could ask him to borrow it to dig out the neighbors, but only after you clear your own walk first.

Dear Cthulhu,

I live in a town that was named after my great, great, great, great, great grandmother, who came to this country with barely any riches and founded the town after having first been granted the rights to the property by the King of England before the Revolutionary War. Over the years it's all been sold off to others until today where I, her last descendant, can't even pay my bills and they want to evict me from my property and sell my house for back taxes.

Since my great, great, great, great, great grandmother once owned all the property in the town, don't I, her great, great, great, great, great granddaughter, have some sort of legal loophole where I can try to claim back the entire town, kind of like the Native Americans have done in some areas?

Then I can kick out all the people who made fun of me over the years and live in peace and quiet with an entire town to myself. How do I go about doing this?

–Descendant who should have Great^5 Grandmother's Land Back

Dear Descendant,

To Cthulhu's knowledge, there is no precedent for ownership to revert if the land had been legally sold. It's different if the land had been leased for a period of time because then you could try to reclaim it although you would be fought along the way. Your best option is to get a job and try to make enough money to pay your taxes before they kick you out. Barring that, try to buy it back for less at auction, making up rumors about the place such as it was built on top of a graveyard, that several murders happened there, that it has radon and asbestos, that your neighbors sell Scamway or essential oils, or that it has no internet or cell phone access. Those are the types of things that will discourage other people from bidding against you.

And should you decide to try anyway, consider this. If you win, it will set a precedent which means other people will do the same thing. Now think about who the British kicked off that land before giving it to your ancestor and realize that then they will simply come and get it back from you.

And unfortunately for you, I did some research and found out that the original natives of your planet had sanctified that land to me well before the start of recorded human history. And since you are of the mind that the land belongs to whomever had it first, consider this your official notice that I am taking possession immediately and am looking for approximately 3.7 million years of back rent. Do not worry, I will allow you three easy payments and will not add any interest provided the pay the balance in full by the time the last payment is due. Do not worry, as I will hold all the humans and businesses in your town equally responsible for paying this debt.

However, should you and the rest of the town default, I will have no other option than to arrive to claim the land and all of you as my property. Best, start putting together the first payment. Or get to work glorifying me by placing art, painting, sculpture and the like glorifying my magnificence. Start by changing the name of the town Cthulhuvale and building me a temple and perhaps I will allow you to go on living your lives without too many changes. And should anyone move out before I foreclose, they will be brought back to for a grand slaughter and souffle night.

Dear Cthulhu,

I'm a teenager living in a small town. My friends and I are perpetually bored out of our minds. There is absolutely nothing to do. The nearest movie theater is like forty minutes away. I'd joke that we stand around watching the traffic light change except we don't even have a real traffic light, just the kind that always blinks so it never changes.

We can even get a decent drink because we're teenagers and underage. Worse, fake IDs wouldn't help because my dad owns the local liquor store and there's no way he's going to let me or my friends buy any booze. We know kids in other places will sometimes use drugs, but we're such a small town we don't even have a drug dealer.

Then my friend "Mario" came up with an idea. He had been reading books from the library–yes, we're so rural we don't even have decent Internet access or a cell phone tower. Most of us still have to use dial–up or satellite. Anyway, these books said that mushrooms were used in vision quests and in the sixties to make people high. We did a bit more research because most of us have eaten mushrooms with food and never noticed feeling any different. It turns out that it's only certain types of mushrooms that have this effect.

Unfortunately, the book doesn't have any pictures of what these particular mushrooms look like. Mario thinks we should all just walk around the woods and the fields picking up any mushrooms we can find so we can try them out. I pointed out that that might be dangerous and he said not to worry, that we'll be fine.

I think it's a bad idea. What do you think? How do we tell mushrooms that'll make us high from the kind we would put on steak?

–Mushroom Hunters In The Sticks

Dear Sticks,

What you are describing is a horrifically dangerous idea, although it might be a cure for boredom, just not in the way you are hoping for. While there are mushrooms that are safe for humans to consume and others that will give humans euphoria and hallucinations, there are even more mushrooms that are poisonous and can do a lot of damage to the human body up to and including death. While death is a cure for boredom it is far worse than the so-called disease.

Cooking mushrooms will do nothing to get rid of their poisonous properties. It's only good for getting rid of bacteria and the like.

Cthulhu will not tell you how to tell the difference between the different types of mushrooms but will point out that it takes most humans quite a bit of extensive training to be able to do so. Also, the type of mushrooms you are hoping to find are not naturally occurring within hundreds of miles of where you live so it is highly unlikely that you will find any, even if you look. If you insist on doing this anyway, try them out on people you do not like in small does first.

Cthulhu recommends trying other ways to relieve your boredom. Use your imagination. Start a business. Play sports or get involved with music or art. Check out books from the library you mentioned. Engage in procreational activities with other townspeople who are interested. Play games, whether they be with cards, on boards, role-playing, or messing with the minds of your fellow humans. Work hard in school so you can go away either to college or trade school and have a profession that will allow you to one day move out of your small town which you find so boring.

Dear Cthulhu,

I read the letter from *Microchipped in Murfreesboro* with interest although he bought into the fake microchip story instead of seeing the real government plot against its own citizens–the plot to turn all pure-blooded American heterosexual males into homosexuals. Obviously, I'm talking about chemtrails. For those among your readers with their heads in the sand, the government regularly seeds the atmosphere via planes, letting chemicals drift down to we the people who live here. Even if they don't directly come in contact with a person, the chemicals can land on crops and get into the water supply. Those chemicals twist every patriotic American man into a mockery. These chemtrails are why there's no record of anyone ever being gay before the Wright brothers flew in 1903. Now Big Rainbow is out there working to make everyone gay and effectively wipe out all of humanity in just a few generations. Well, I for one won't stand for it, because I've become a victim of Big Rainbow. It happened a few months back when I went to an air show. Had I only known about the chemtrails then, my life would not have been destroyed as it was.

The highlight of the show was when the crack fighter jet squad, the Green Devils, flew in formation over the show. It was something to see. Those pilots were amazing. Unfortunately, they left their monstrous trail behind them to fall on those of us in the crowd.

To be truthful I didn't feel anything right away. I was tailgating and camping nearby and I'll admit I got more than a little drunk. That's the other thing they don't tell you–alcohol use speeds up the reaction of chemtrail toxins. When it started raining, the falling water pushed even more of the poison down from the sky onto my skin, but, good old boy that I am, I wasn't about to let a little rain dampen my spirits or stop me from getting my party on.

The rain became a storm then turned practically into a monsoon, There was lightning and thunder everywhere and we were all outside in the open. I was camping in a tent next to my pickup, but the storm had knocked it over. It was hanging by just a couple of stakes.

I'd been tailgating with this guy "Van" who'd I just met at the show who offered to let me ride out the storm in his RV. It seemed like it'd be a lot more comfortable than sitting in the cab of my pickup so I said sure.

The day had been hot and humid but the rain had brought the temperature down quite a bit. He'd left the AC on in his RV so when we stepped inside we were soaked to the bone and freezing. Van suggested I get out of my wet clothes, and he did the same. Let me tell, you this guy had muscles on top of muscles and skin like porcelain. I'd always admired the male physique, but I'd never been alone with one while both of us were wearing just undies and socks. I had on boxers but Van was wearing little bikini briefs. I could not stop from imagining what he would look like if they fell off. Or if I tore them off with my teeth.

Van must've saw me staring. I felt kind of awkward but he just smiled. He asked me if I was still cold. I admitted I was. Van suggested that I jump into his shower to warm up a bit. He failed to mention that he would be coming in behind me. The shower was very small and barely had enough room for two of us. I started to say something but then he turned on the hot water and started sudsing up my back. Then he dug in deep and massaged my sore muscles. It felt very good and I was about to tell Van that I wasn't gay when he rubbed himself up against my back and reached around to start washing my front.

I was raised to be a gentleman. Van was my host after all and I didn't want to offend him by being rude, so I let him finish soaping me up although he did pay close attention to one certain part, if you get my drift. Again, not wanting to be rude I returned the favor. Things got out of hand and into other places. Before you know it, we made sweet passionate love. I'd never done such a thing with anyone before the chemtrails. I was feeling awkward and guilty, wondering what my family and friends would say. I got up to begin my walk of shame but Van pulled me back in the bed. It was still storming out and my tent wasn't the safest place to be, assuming it was still even there so I stayed.

I started to point out that we shouldn't do this because I wasn't gay but Van quieted me with a sweet and tender kiss. One thing led to another yet again and once again we made with the lovemaking. This time we both fell asleep. When I woke up in the morning, it was bright and sunny. I got out of bed to make a second attempt at my walk of shame, but Van woke, rushed after me and lifted me up on his shoulder. He tossed me on the bed and started tickling me. He invited me to have some dessert after which we ate breakfast, if you catch my drift.

So as you can see the chemtrail turned me gay. I want to know if I can sue the government. Although I'd be happy to take a few million or so for my trouble I'm more interested in a cure of some sort. I mean the government would not do something like this unless they could undo it, right?

What's worse, I haven't had the heart to tell "Barbara," my girlfriend of eight years what I'd done because we have not yet made the sweet, sweet love as I told her I was waiting for marriage. To be honest I wasn't all that motivated despite her constant tries at seduction with the blatant dirty talk, kinky offers, and constant parading of herself in lingerie. I suspect that if Barbara were to find out she'd be very cross with me.

I live in a small town and really don't want my experience as a chemtrail victim to become feed for the town's gossip mill. I haven't told anyone about what Van and I are doing. Yes, I am still doing the gay with Van because I just don't want to hurt the man's feelings. I think he'd be devastated if I if we stopped. Plus, I feel my family and friends might disown me even though being gay is not my fault but the chemtrails'.

How can I fix this?

–Straight Man Doing The Gay In Gainesville

Dear Doing,

I have some good and possibly devastating news for you. There is no truth to the rumor that the government is making people gay using chemtrails. You have always been gay and just not allowed yourself to acknowledge this aspect of you. It is likely why you have not tried to procreate with your girlfriend, despite eight years of her coming on to you, yet you jump into a travel bed with the first guy who offered to shower with you. It was likely due to a mixture of having the opportunity while your inhibitions were lowered by excessive alcohol consumption with a little adrenaline from the storm that was raging thrown in for good measure.

Being gay or hetero or bisexual or asexual has no innate goodness or badness. It is just humans working to fulfill their primal need for procreation. And as Cthulhu has stated many times before, I have to look very closely at many of you lot to tell the difference between all your genders, races, and body types. There are those who would tell you to seek counseling in order to accept who you are, which is largely a huge waste of time and money. Deep down you know what kind of person you are, so embrace it and don't allow others to make you feel less than because you're no less than any other human. You are all a very pathetic lot as a whole. Ultimately there is no point trying to change or fix yourself. Like every other human, you are broken, although that degree of breakage can vary greatly. Be like Cthulhu and be proud of what you are, even if it is just a lowly human. Embrace it.

Plus there is no true way to change this although humans

have tried. One of the eviller actions your society has come up with is so-called conversion therapy which is simply people using their religious beliefs as an excuse to torture others to come around to their point of view. The irony is if they truly read their holy books they would realize that they're doing the exact opposite of what the books outline as preferred behavior. In truth, the only religion that should be allowed to torture other humans to come around to the correct point of view is of course the Cult of Cthulhu and most of that torture should be done by me or my direct designates. In fact, much of it is now available on Cthulhu's Lonely Fans channel. Cult members get 50% off the first 3 months of their subscription. Be sure to use code HURTMECTHULHU at checkout.

End your relationship with your girlfriend so as to allow her to find someone who can give her what she wants. Discuss with your procreational partner Van and others how they deal with the difficulties posed by the prejudices of some in your society. Consider relocating to a place that would be more accepting of your procreational choices.

Dear Cthulhu,

My wife "Jezebel" recently found out I was cheating on her with her sister. To be honest, technically I feel I'm cheating on her sister with her. My wife and I were high school sweethearts, but she never gave me any and told me she wouldn't give it up until we were married.

Jezebel's making up for that now, but I'll get to that in a bit. I'd hoped that prom night might be the night Jezebel changed her mind, but nope, just a kiss after, and then telling me to take her home. So I did but as I was walking back to my car, her sister "Minx" waved at me from her room on the ground floor. I went over to her window and when Minx stepped out from behind the curtain, she was totally naked. Minx invited me into her room and gave me everything that her sister wouldn't.

The simple truth is that even in high school, my wife was happier "going out" on dates rather than "putting out" afterward. Even married, she rarely wanted to do anything more than make out. Her sister on the other hand didn't want anything resembling a relationship, just booty calls whenever she needed it, which was often. For six and a half glorious years, it's been the ideal situation. My wife was the perfect girlfriend then the perfect wife, working full time at night and still cleaning and cooking and taking care of all the household needs. When she went out to work, her sister would come over and take care of my more physical needs. I thought it would last forever until I was undone by the damn flu.

My wife got sick at work then came home to find me in bed with her sister. Although technically we weren't in bed but on a couple of trapeze–style sling swings that I had set up in the bedroom. I'd hidden the hooks for them behind light fixtures so my wife never noticed but oh boy did she notice that night.

Jezebel was furious. My foot got caught in the swing when I tried to get away. I ended up dangling helplessly upside down as she beat me senseless with a spatula like I was a naked piñata. I guess I should count myself lucky as she'd been originally reaching for a steak knife and was so upset she just stuck with what she'd grabbed.

Between beatings, Jezebel asked how long things had been going on with Minx. Of course, I did the smart thing and said this was the first time but her twit of a sister told her the truth, that we'd been hooking up ever since the night of our prom.

Jezebel swore she'd get even with me by sleeping with every guy she met from then on. I thought she was exaggerating as I passed out from all the blows to my head.

She wasn't. I came home one night from work and found the house a mess. Instead of dinner on the kitchen table, my wife was on it with a couple of guys. I tried to beat them up, but there were two of them and it didn't do so well, so I called 911. I wanted charges pressed, but the cop let them go, saying that my wife had invited them there and she had that right since she lived there. Jezebel thanked the cop by taking him into our bedroom and showing him new uses for his handcuffs and baton. He even let her keep his hat and the cuffs.

I laid down the law and told her I'd stop making mortgage payments on the house and move out if that happened again. In our state, in a divorce the wife gets half of everything, regardless of adultery. I make over two hundred grand a year and she works at a buck over minimum wage. It's not exactly going to be an equitable distribution of assets. At least not from my point of view.

Jezebel took my threats to heart and now goes out every night. She calls a Zuber and doesn't even pay for them, at least not with money if you get my drift. I didn't realize that until I called a Zuber. When the guy picked me up, he asked me why I got in the back seat. He had his pants down around his ankles and when he turned around was shocked to see that I wasn't my wife. That's when I realized that the line of cars across the street from our house wasn't just people parked but a line of Zuber drivers waiting for my wife to take them for a ride.

I found out she's got this thing now where she meets guys on hook–up apps like Humper, tells them to wear a red carnation, and does them right in the parking outside the bar where she meets them.

I can't take it anymore. If she'd shown a tenth of this enthusiasm with me, I never would've slept with her sister in the first place. Worse, Minx feels guilty since we got caught and won't sleep with me anymore, saying it would be disrespectful to her sister. I asked her what about all the years we'd been messing around decade and she said that was different because her sister didn't know then.

My wife has said she won't sign a legal separation agreement, and that I will have to go for the full divorce. I worked too hard for everything I have just to give half of it to her. What can I do?

–Husband With The Tables Turned In Albuquerque

Dear Turned,

Like most humans, you have no one to blame for your current situation but yourself. You knew your wife was not as interested in procreational activities as you were, yet you married her anyway. Then you repeatedly broke your wedding vows with her sibling. As she is now repeatedly breaking your wedding vows as well, that appears to be a wash.

Jezebel is hurt and trying to cause you emotional pain in return. Since you don't even mention the possibility of counseling and reconciliation, you will have to live with the situation as it is now or go ahead and get the divorce. You may want to hold off long enough for you to hide some of your more liquid assets in offshore accounts and then wait a few months before you officially file, because as Cthulhu understands it once you go before the courts all your accounts will be monitored and you will not be able to move any of your assets. As your wife is going to get half of anything you are unable to hide, your best bet is to find the meanest, toughest divorce attorney in your town and hire them to represent you. Then hire the next half–dozen for some unrelated matter so it would be a conflict of interest for them to take your wife's case against you. If she is smart, she will then go out of town for representation.

Of course, in these cases, the judges can always rule and give one party more than half if they see fit. As your wife would seem to have no issues influencing the judge with her procreational prowess, you had best hope for a female or gay judge.

Or you could become a Zuber driver in disguise and hope for the best.

Dear Cthulhu,

I'm a drag queen. I know in this day and age some people don't like that term, but I'm a 45-year-old queen and I've been doing this since I was 16 so I'll call myself whatever I damn well please, thank you very much.

I've never gotten rich, but I've always managed to make a living performing. I even had a single that made the Top 200 on the Nillboard Charts. For the last decade, I've made my living at a club called *The Drag Races*. I live in a town that's big on racing from stock cars to PASKAR. We even have a track.

Theater performances have suffered lately. I blame the internet and Reality TV. With entertainment on their phones, folks just don't go out to see live theater as much as they did when I was starting out, so business has fallen off. Besides all we do is act, sing, and dance and there are a few other clubs in town where they do a lot more than that. Things that, as an artist, I am not willing to do.

One day my boss Priscilla got what she thought was a great idea. Given the name of her establishment and the fact that she drove stock cars on the weekends, she decided that we should have our own weekly "drag" races at the local track. She was friends with the owner and managed to get permission and a permit. That in and of itself was an accomplishment. Except for Priscilla, none of us girls at the club were professional drivers, so we had to get an amateur permit for the track which means that anybody can drive. We also have to carry a higher insurance premium but in the end, it meant that theoretically anybody who wanted could be allowed to race.

Cthulhu darling, the first few weeks were simply fabulous. We did a show before and between races and charged for tickets.

By the third week, we were selling out the track. Admittedly it's not a huge arena, but we were making as much in one race as we were for a week of singing and dancing in the club. And our drag races were on Tuesday nights, which was traditionally a dead club night, anyway. And the "drag races" were so hot we started filling the club on the other nights.

It sounds like everything was absolutely marvelous, right? It was, until some of the culture–impaired race fans in town found out about us having the amateur permit. Then–no tea, no shade– it got uglier than the clearance rack at the Salvation Navy. These wannabes started lining up and demanding their right to race on the track under our permit and turn our Glamazon racing extravaganza into a bar king night.

When Priscilla told them no, they started claiming discrimination, which made us pause. Being against discrimination is a subject near and dear to our hearts. So many of us gals have been, and still are, discriminated against in everyday life that we're loathe to do it, even unintentionally, to the uncouth masses. At the same time, we don't want to let the crudees race during our time either. It would ruin the show. They can do what we did and make a boring race night of their own. We aren't stopping them.

What can we do?

–Fast and Fabulous in Fox Lake

Dear Fabulous,

Rules are rules. Humans should follow rules. Cthulhu is worshiped and glorified as the be all and end all by the Cult of Cthulhu. My followers need to follow the rules of my church without question or I end up spending too much time disciplining them which tends to thin out their numbers and lower the weekly tithes. Therefore, other humans need to follow rules and maintain their vows in order to set a good example for my worshippers. The last thing any religion needs is people believing that they can think for themselves without consequences. Plus, my time is too valuable. If I had to consistently reign in and punish worshippers, I would miss my weekly mahjong game and gain weight from devouring all the bodies which would wreak havoc on Cthulhu's sexy figure and make my face tentacles all pudgy. So if the rules on this amateur permit state that anyone should be allowed to race, then you must allow them to race.

However, you may also enforce your own rules and have some fun doing so, inspired by their "cries" of discrimination.

You have already established that it is a "drag" race, namely a contest where the drivers must dress as women even if they are males. (Understand that human gender and the fuss involved means little to Cthulhu. I do not understand the issue as most humans look the same to me. Why should it matter to anyone if a person is male, female, or another option? You should be more focused on the shame of being human and support each other against the rest of the universe which only desires your unavoidable deaths and inevitable destruction.)

Simply insist that if a person wants to race they must follow the rules. Make a new one that allows you to pick the new drivers' outfits. Also, since all current drivers participate in the show, any newcomers must do the same. As a show person with almost three decades of experience, I expect that on more than one occasion you have had the opportunity to bring someone from the audience up on stage and have some fun with them. Do the same with these would-be racers.

Knowing what the drivers will have to do to drive will likely mean the new drivers' friends and family will hear about it and undoubtedly buy tickets to watch them perform, which will only help sales. Only allow one new racer a week, which will provide your show with a stream of fresh performers. Perhaps you may even help a human who does not have the courage to show their true selves as you do, come out of the cupboard as they say. Maybe some will even have talent and you will get new performers for the club.

You can even record the performances and put them on Klik Klok to promote the races, the clubs, and maybe bring in some extra income.

Dear Cthulhu,

I have been a grifter since I could walk. My mother would fill up my onesies when we went into a store and have me walk out with whatever merchandise could fit. By the time she abandoned me on my eighth birthday, I'd learned to grift on my own, so I didn't starve.

I've been grifting ever since. My favorite time of year is Christmas. Sometimes I don't even have to grift because people give out free food and stuff. This year I came up with a new con. I set up my own Salvation Navy donation pot and rang a bell all day while dressed as Kris Kringle. It was almost like working a real job but it wasn't technically illegal because I didn't put the name of the charity on the red pot so people were just handing over their money to me. I never even asked. I just stood there in the red and white Santa Claus outfit with the fake beard and rang a bell. The best part was if anyone complained, the Santa beard hid my face from any video cameras and the Santa gloves stopped me from leaving any fingerprints.

It was the perfect scam.

I made thousands and paid my rent three months in advance, bought clothes without holes in them, and filled up my freezer and kitchen with a few months' worth of food.

After all that, I still had eleven grand and was going out to party, still dressed up in the red and white. Some women have a kink thing for Santa you know.

On the way to a bar, I stopped to relieve myself in an alley and heard a couple of kids crying. It turns out that they and their parents had been kicked out of their apartment a few weeks before and were homeless. The kids, a boy and a girl, were upset that Santa wouldn't be able to find them. It turns out that when they sat on his lap to tell him what they wanted they asked him to give their parents enough money to pay their bills. They were worried that because they weren't in their house, Santa wouldn't be able to find them to give their parents the gift they asked for.

The parents were trying to tell the kids it was okay, that the most important part of Christmas was that they were still together. I've got to tell you, that hit me in a place I didn't even know I had. My family never cared squat about me except for what they could use me to steal. And here were these people who had nothing except each other and damn me if it wasn't beautiful.

Without thinking, I stepped out from behind the dumpster where I had answered nature's call yelling, "Ho, ho, ho."

The kids yelled that it was Santa Claus, and the parents began to look nervous. I told them I had a little trouble locating them but finally tracked them down. I handed each of the kids five hundred bucks and gave the rest—ten grand—to their parents. There was a lot of crying, some of it by me, followed by hugging and thank yous. Then the family went off to find a hotel for the night and I was left eleven grand poorer but feeling better inside than I ever had in my life.

I still feel good when I should feel like a sucker. I mean, I gave these total strangers my entire bankroll but instead of feeling like a fool, I feel happy.

What's wrong with me?

–Phony Santa in Sacramento

Dear Phony,

Technically, there is nothing wrong with you per se. There is a defect in the human brain whereby doing good deeds and helping others can release endorphins which makes people feel good because they did good. Much of your society has designated late December as a time for helping others and being kind without cause. It is the one time of year humanity is almost tolerable. Some credit a higher authority but as I am a religious rival, I am loath to give any credit to my competition, especially if it is deserved. Cthulhu will not even get into all his resentment that *Cthulhumas* has not caught on despite the efforts of my most loyal disciple.

Do not worry, eventually the endorphins will wear off and you will get to choose to continue to help others or revert to your selfish ways. I suspect it will be the latter.

But you should not feel too bad because last Christmas Eve even the magnificent Cthulhu himself fell prey to this disgusting holiday.

My worshipers had scheduled a potluck and ritual sacrifice on Christmas Eve. It made sense as most of them had the next day off from work and could sleep in.

I was busy preparing for the night of adoration and snacks when I noticed a young girl in my worship chamber. Oddly, she did not notice me and began to play with a stuffed toy–a plushie that was made to resemble handsome Cthulhu. Together she and the stuffed me that she called Tully (the human child spoke with a lisp) played, had tea, and pretended to conquer the world. I found it quite adorable.

When she finally noticed me, I prepared for the screams of terror and horror I have come to expect from the young. Instead, the girl grinned, ran up, and hugged me. It caught Cthulhu off guard. Few humans dare approach me and fewer still willingly touch me.

The surprises continued when she asked me to join in her human games. We then pretended to conquer the world and the child surprised me with several good insights that I wrote down to use at a later date. This was followed by imaginary tea.

The child hugged me goodbye and turned to leave, but instead stopped to stare. I was a little disappointed as she had not displayed any issues with my appearance prior.

It turned out that I had misjudged the child. She said that Cthulhu looked lonely, so she gave me the stuffed version of myself, then told me that Tully would help me not be so lonely.

Cthulhu never thanks anyone, yet I found myself thanking her.

Later that evening, after some lovely snacks and one scrumptious Sriracha peppermint kitten soufflé, it was sacrifice time. Lo and behold, who did they bring out the sacrifice to me but that same little girl.

There are some things so heinous and unspeakable that even Cthulhu will not partake or condone. To make a long and gory story short, instead of one, there were three sacrifices that Christmas Eve. Two were the child's parents and one was the DHS (Director of Human Sacrifices). The girl now has a much safer home and has made it onto my Cthulhumas card list. I kept Tully.

It truly was a Merry Cthulhumas.

Have A Dark Day.

There has long been a debate among certain obscure and drunken literary scholars about whether **PATRICK THOMAS** was raised by Cthulhu, a leprechaun in a Manhattan bar, or two human parents. What there is no arguing about is that Patrick is the award-winning author of 40 books including the beloved fantasy humor *Murphy's Lore series* (9 books from *Tales from Bulfinche's Pub* to *The Mug Life*), as well as 2 books in the future space adventures in the *Startenders* series.

The Murphy's Lore After Hours spin-offs star the half pixie/ogre Terrorbelle (*Fairy With A Gun, Fairy Rides The Lightning,* and *Terrorbelle The Unconquered*); the former demon-possessed serial killer Agent Karver of the Department of Mystic Affairs (*Dead To Rites, Rites of Passage*); the cursed magí Hex (*By Darkness Cursed* and *By Invocation Only*); Vince Argus, the Soul For Hire (*Greatest Hits*); and Negral, a forgotten Sumerian god who works as Hell's Detective (*Lore & Dysorder, Bullets & Brimstone,* and the graphic novel *The Moon Maniac* with Blair Webb).

His *Mystic Investigators* paranormal mystery series includes *Shadows & Brimstone* (omnibus of *Bullets & Brimstone* and *From The Shadows* with John L. French), *Once Upon In Crime* (omnibus of *Once More Upon A Time* and *Partners In Crime* with Diane Raetz) *Mystic Investigators,* and *Mean Streets. Assassins' Ball* is his first traditional mystery, co-written with John L. French. He co-edited *Camelot 13, New Blood, Hear Them Roar* and was an editor for the magazines *Fantastic Stories of the Imagination* and *Pirate Writings*.

His other works include the steampunk *As The Gears Turn.* the space epic *Exile & Entrance*, and the *Bikini Jones* series. Patrick's darkly humorous advice column *Dear Cthulhu* has been running since 2005 and has 6 collections including *Cthulhu Knows Best* and *What Would Cthulhu Do?* The Dear Cthulhu advice empire has expanded from magazines and books to radio as Dear Cthulhu now broadcasts monthly on the show Destinies: The Voice of Science Fiction which is hosted by Dr. Howard Margolin.

Over 100 of his stories have been published in magazines and anthologies. His noir novella appears in *Murder in Montague Falls*. A number of his books were part of the props department of the *CSI* television show and *Nightcaps* was even thrown at a suspect's head. His urban fantasy *Fairy With A Gun* had been optioned for film and TV by Laurence Fishburne's Cinema Gypsy Productions. Top Men Productions has turned his *Soul For Hire* Story, *Act of Contrition*, into a short film.

He also writes books for kids as PATRICK T. FIBBS including the YA *Emotional Support Nightmare*, the midde readers U*ndead Kid Diaries: Over My Dead Body,* the *Babe B. Bear Mysteries: Bad Hair Day, Joy Reaper Checks Out,* the picture book *Fushcia The Mermaid Who Loved Pink*, and *the Ughabooz* picture books *5 Silly Monsters Jumping On The Zed* and *On Top Of A Yeti*, and the early reader *Soggy Goes to the Beach*.

Please drop by www.patthomas.net or follow him at I_PatrickThomas at Twitter or www.facebook.com/PatrickThomasAuthor to learn more.

**Being _CURSED_ to wear a bikini
Won't stop this Hero
From _SAVING_ the world**

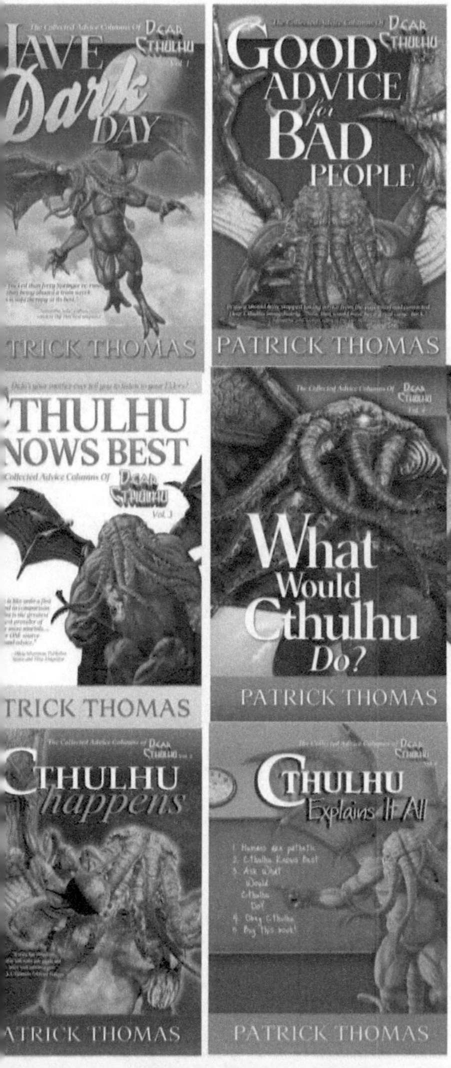

DEAR CTHULHU

**THE ADVICE
COLUMN TO
END ALL
ADVICE COLUMNS**

Welcome to the Freakshow!
Monsters Among Us
a Bianca Jones collection

PAST SINS

Bad Cop...
No Donut

THE GREY MONK
SOULS ON FIRE
JOHN L. FRENCH

Welcome to Baltimore!
e There Be ONSTERS
a Bianca Jones collection
JOHN L. FRENCH

THE NIGHT MARE STRIKES
"THE NIGHTMARE IS COOL"
-MICHAEL A. BLACK, AUTHOR
OF CRIMES AT MIDNIGHT
AND THE EXECUTIONER SERIES
JOHN L. FRENCH

IT'S A CRIME
TO MISS THESE
GREAT STORIES!
from author
John L. French

WWW.PADWOLF.COM

You can't get better than 13!

APOCALYPSE 13
THIRTEEN FANTASTICAL
TALES FOR THE END OF DAYS
DEFCON

TALES FROM THE SEA
MERMAIDS 13

Celebrating the spirit of Arthur and His Knights
Camelot 13
Edited by
John L. French and Patrick Thomas

EDITED BY EDWARD J. McFADDEN
LUCKY 13
Thirteen Tales of Crime & Mayhem

FUTURES
ANTHOLOGY

DOWN THESE MEAN STREETS
of Magic & Monsters walk the

MYSTIC INVESTIGATORS